Animal.

CALF

LUCY DANIELS

Calf
Capers

Illustrated by Paul Howard

a division of Hodder Headline Limited

Special thanks to Narinder Dhami

Text copyright © 2002 Working Partners Limited,
Created by Working Partners Limited, London W6 OQT
Illustrations copyright © 2002 Paul Howard
Cover illustration by Chris Chapman

First published in Great Britain in 2002
by Hodder Children's Books

A Catalogue record for this book is available
from the British Library

ISBN 0 340 85205 4

Typeset by Avon Dataset Ltd, Bidford-on-Avon, Warks

Printed and bound in Great Britain by
The Guernsey Press Co. Ltd, Channel Isles

Hodder Children's Books
a division of Hodder Headline Limited
338 Euston Road
London NW1 3BH

Contents

1

A very special delivery

"Hurry up, Dad!" Mandy Hope said eagerly. "I can't *wait* to see Jenny. Do you think she's had her calf yet?"

Mandy's dad smiled as he drove the Land-rover along the winding country road. "I don't know, love," he replied. "We'll just have to wait and see."

It was a sunny Saturday morning in June, and

Mandy and Mr Hope were on their way to Treetop Farm, which was owned by Mike Talbot. One of Mike's cows, Jenny, was about to give birth to a new calf. Mandy's dad was a vet, and Mike had asked him to come along in case there were any problems. Mandy had been thrilled when her dad had said she could come too – she'd never seen a calf being born before.

"Look, Dad!" Mandy pointed at a poster stuck on a wooden pole at the side of the road. It was for the local agricultural show, which was being held in Welford in three weeks' time. "My whole class is going to the show," Mandy went on excitedly. "And so is James's." James Hunter was Mandy's best friend. "We're doing a project about it. Everyone has to choose one thing at the show to write about."

"That sounds interesting," said Mr Hope. "And it looks like Jenny's calf is going to arrive just in time. I know that Mike wants to enter Jenny and her calf in one of the classes at the show."

"What kind of breed is Jenny?" Mandy asked.

"She's a Dexter cow," Mr Hope explained, as he turned off the road, down a narrow lane.

"Dexters aren't kept in big herds any more because they're very small, so they don't produce much milk. Mike and his wife just have Jenny because they're interested in keeping the breed going."

"I've never seen a Dexter cow before," Mandy said.

"Well, Jenny's a fine example," her dad told her. "She and her calves have won the prize at the show for the last two years. Mike and Rachel are very proud of her."

Jenny must be a very special cow, Mandy thought. She was really looking forward to seeing her. Mandy was mad about animals. She thought she was really lucky that *both* of her parents were vets – it meant that there were always lots of different animals to meet.

Mr Hope drove past a sign saying *Treetop Farm*, then he pulled into a large, square farmyard. A few hens were scratching in the dusty earth, but they hurried out of the way as the Land-rover drew to a halt.

Mandy looked around with interest. She'd never been to the Talbots' farm before. The farmhouse was a long, white-painted cottage with a thatched roof, and next to it were a large stone barn and several smaller cowsheds.

As Mandy and Mr Hope climbed out of the Land-rover, the farmhouse door opened. A short woman with fair hair came out and hurried over to them. "Hello, Adam," she said. She turned and smiled at Mandy. "And you must be Mandy. I've heard a lot about you! I'm Rachel Talbot, Mike's wife."

"Hello, Rachel. How's Jenny?" asked Mr Hope, lifting his bag out of the back of the Land-rover.

"She's fine," replied Mrs Talbot. "We've been checking on her regularly, but this is her third calf, so she knows what she's doing!"

At that moment, a tall, stockily-built man with a cheerful face came out of one of the barns. "Adam, good to see you." He came forward to shake Mr Hope's hand. "And I can guess who this is. Hello, Mandy."

Mandy smiled at him. "Hello."

"I've just looked in on Jenny again," Mike went on, as he led them over to the biggest barn. "She's lying down, but she seems quite comfortable."

Mandy followed Mike, her father and Mrs Talbot into the barn. Her heart was thumping with excitement. Mike took them over to a pen, and there was Jenny, lying on a bed of straw. Her sides heaved, and every so often she gave a big, puffing sigh.

"Hello, Jenny," Mandy said softly. The cow was much smaller than the black and white cows that Mandy was used to. She was a pretty, reddish-brown colour, and she had two short, sharp-looking horns on top of her head. Her eyes were large and dark as she stared up at Mandy.

"Wait here, Mandy," said Mr Hope, as he and Mike went inside the pen. Mandy stood watching with Mrs Talbot while her dad examined Jenny. He ran his hands over her sides and listened to her chest with a stethoscope.

"She's doing fine," said Mr Hope. "It won't be long now."

Mandy leaned over the side of the pen, her gaze fixed on Jenny. Suddenly the cow gave a long, low moo and lifted her tail. Mandy's eyes widened as she saw the calf's tiny hooves begin to appear. "Good girl, Jenny!" she whispered.

The hooves were quickly followed by the calf's nose and head. Mandy watched excitedly, hardly daring to breathe, as the calf's damp little body slipped on to the straw.

"Well done, Jenny," said Mike. He and his wife were both smiling with delight. "And the calf's another beauty, by the look of it."

Mr Hope wiped some sticky liquid out of the calf's nostrils. "It's a little girl," he announced.

The calf lay in a heap, blinking her big, brown eyes. She was exactly the same reddish-brown colour as her mum, and Mandy thought she was *gorgeous*. She had a round, furry face, just like a teddy bear!

Jenny pushed herself up on to her feet. She looked a bit unsteady at first, but she finally made it. Then she began to clean her calf's damp coat, licking and licking with her long pink tongue.

"Jenny looks very proud of her new baby," Mandy said, her eyes shining. It had been brilliant to watch the calf being born.

Mike turned to her. "Would you like to give Jenny's calf a name, Mandy?" he asked.

"Oh, can I?" Mandy gasped. She gazed at the calf, wondering what to call her. Rosie? Molly? No, the calf just didn't *look* like a Rosie, or a Molly.

Mandy thought hard. "What about Tilly?" she suggested shyly, at last.

"Jenny and Tilly," Mike said thoughtfully. "Perfect! What do you think, Rachel?"

"I think she looks just like a Tilly," laughed his wife.

Jenny had finished cleaning Tilly now, and Mr Hope stepped forward to listen to her chest again. Meanwhile, Tilly was trying to climb to her feet. She pushed herself up on to her back legs first, so that her bottom stuck in the air. Then she used her front hooves to lever herself upright. Mandy watched anxiously as the calf's long legs skittered in all directions. For a moment or two, it looked as if Tilly was going to topple over. But finally she managed to stand up, her legs wobbling underneath her.

"Clever girl, Tilly!" Mandy exclaimed. Calves were so clever. Tilly was only a few minutes old, but already she was on her feet!

Tilly took a few careful steps forward. She staggered a little, but then got her balance. Lowering her little head, she began to drink her mother's milk.

"Tilly's first drink of milk is very important," Mr Hope told Mandy. "There are special vitamins in it which will help her grow up strong and healthy."

Tilly sucked happily, her damp little tail flicking from side to side in delight. Meanwhile,

Mandy saw that Jenny had spotted the rack of hay at the side of the pen. The cow could just about reach it without moving away from Tilly. Jenny stretched her neck forward, took a big mouthful of hay and began to chew.

Mike and his wife burst out laughing. "That's typical of Jenny!" Mike grinned. "She's the greediest cow we've ever owned."

"She must be hungry after working so hard," Mandy said. "Is Jenny OK, Dad?"

"She's fine," replied Mr Hope.

Mandy turned as she heard the sound of a car entering the farmyard. Mike looked round too, and clapped a hand to his forehead. "Oh, I nearly forgot!" he said. "The *Walton Gazette* are coming to take a picture of Tilly. That's probably them now."

"Tilly's the hundredth calf born on our farm," Mrs Talbot explained, "so that makes her even more special."

"Did you hear that, Tilly?" Mandy said. The calf raised her head and stared at Mandy with her huge eyes. "You're the most special calf on the whole farm!"

Mike slipped out of the barn and came back

a few moments later with a tall, dark-haired woman. She had a camera round her neck and a notebook in her hand.

"Hi, Rachel," she called, with a wave.

"Alison, this is our vet, Adam Hope, and his daughter Mandy," Mrs Talbot said. "This is Alison West. She's a reporter on the *Walton Gazette*, and an old schoolfriend of mine."

"I phoned her when I knew Tilly was on the way," explained Mike. "Thanks for coming so quickly, Alison."

"Not at all." Alison grinned. "It's a nice change from taking pictures of weddings!" She leaned over the pen and looked in at Tilly, who'd finished feeding and was standing close to her mum's side. "Isn't she gorgeous? Our readers are going to love her. Can I take some photos now?"

Mike nodded, and Alison turned to Mandy. "I'd like you to be in the picture too," she said. "Mandy, would you stand next to Tilly, and stroke her? Is that OK, Mike?"

"Sure," said Mike. "Just go in very quietly, Mandy. Jenny won't mind."

"OK, Mr Talbot," Mandy said, feeling

thrilled. Not only had she seen her first calf being born, but now she was going to have her photo in the newspaper, along with Jenny and Tilly. Mandy couldn't *wait* to see James and tell him all about it!

2

Front page news!

Mike opened the pen and Mandy went in as quietly as she could, so that she didn't alarm Jenny or Tilly. She stood next to Tilly, feeling the calf's warm little body pressed against her legs. Tilly's short hair felt very soft, and her skin was warm and wrinkly, as if she still had to grow into it. Tilly seemed a bit nervous and edged closer to her mum, but she let Mandy pat her little head, and softly stroke her reddish-brown back.

Mike reached over the side of the pen and rubbed Jenny's head to keep her calm.

"Right, let's see a nice big smile, Mandy," said Alison, lifting her camera. "You too, Jenny and Tilly!"

Mike took his hand away, and Jenny let out a very loud moo, which made Mandy laugh. Alison took a couple of photos, and then everyone left the pen.

"I think Jenny and Tilly deserve some peace and quiet," said Mike, as they went out of the barn into the summer sunshine. Mandy turned and took one last glance at Tilly. The calf had flopped down on to the straw, snuggled close against her mother's side, and looked as if she was already snoozing.

"Mike, I'd like to ask you a few questions so I can write a short article to go with the photo," said Alison as they crossed the farm-yard. "Would that be OK? I know you're busy."

Mike nodded. "We're making hay like mad while this fine weather lasts," he said. "But I

can spare a few minutes."

"Why don't we all go into the kitchen and have a cup of tea?" suggested Mrs Talbot, glancing at Mandy and her dad. "If you're not in a hurry, Adam."

"That would be lovely," Mandy's dad agreed.

"Good." Mrs Talbot beamed. "I've made a big fruit cake, and some gingerbread."

"Oh, yum!" Mandy said, and blushed as everyone laughed.

The farmhouse kitchen was large and comfortable, with a big pine table and a ginger cat asleep on a sagging armchair. A delicious smell of freshly-baked cakes hung in the air.

"Let's get started straight away, Mike," said Alison. She sat down at the table and uncapped her pen. "How did you get interested in rare breeds like Jenny?"

"A friend of mine owned a Dexter cow once, and that's how I got to know about them," replied Mike. Mandy, who was stroking the ginger cat, listened with interest. "I think that farmers ought to make an effort to keep rare breeds going. If we don't, they die out, and then they're lost for ever."

Alison nodded and jotted down a few notes. "So will you be entering Jenny and Tilly in the local agricultural show this year?" she asked.

"Of course!" Mike grinned. "Jenny has done very well in the past with her previous calves, and, hopefully, Tilly's going to be just the same."

"And is your brother entering his Dexter cow this year again, too?" Alison went on.

Mike shrugged. "I'm not sure," he said. "You'll have to ask him that."

Mandy wondered who Mike's brother was. She didn't know any other farmers called Talbot.

"Tea's ready." Rachel carried the tray over to the table, and put it down. "Mandy, would you like some gingerbread?"

"Yes, please," Mandy said, and grinned as Mrs Talbot handed her a huge slice.

"So how do you feel about competing against your brother, Mike?" asked Alison, spooning some sugar into her tea. "I believe your Jenny has beaten his cow for the last couple of years."

"Well, it'll be a fair class, as usual," replied Mike, as he reached for a piece of fruitcake.

"I'm sure the best cow will win!"

Mandy hoped that would be Jenny. She'd never seen Jenny's other calves, but surely they couldn't have been prettier than Tilly.

"I must get back to the haymaking." Mike drained his teacup and stood up. "Nice to see you again, Alison. Thanks for coming, Adam, and you too, Mandy."

"Thank you for letting me see Tilly," Mandy said with a big smile. "She's lovely."

The farmer's blue eyes twinkled. "I can see that you've fallen in love with her!" he remarked, as he went over to put his boots on. "If you want to pop over and visit Tilly next week, you're very welcome. Bring a friend, if you like."

"Oh, thank you!" Mandy exclaimed. "I'll bring James. He'd *love* to meet Tilly."

Mike went out, and Alison got to her feet too. "I've got to get back to work," she said. She smiled at Mandy. "Look out for the photo. It'll be in Friday's edition of the paper."

"I will!" Mandy said eagerly. She was already planning to cut out the picture and stick it in her scrapbook.

"Thanks for the tea, Rachel." Adam Hope reached for his bag. "Come on, Mandy. We'd better be going."

"Dad, could I say goodbye to Jenny and Tilly before we go?" Mandy asked. She just wanted *one* more look at the beautiful little calf before they left.

"All right, if you're quick," her dad replied with a smile.

They said goodbye to Mrs Talbot, and Mandy

went across to the barn while her dad put his bag in the Land-rover. She peered in through the open door. Jenny and Tilly were lying on the straw in their pen, cuddled close together. They looked sleepy and comfortable.

"Bye, Jenny," Mandy whispered. "Bye, Tilly." Then she hurried over to join her dad.

"How are they?" asked Mr Hope, as Mandy climbed into the Land-rover.

"A bit tired, I think," Mandy said. "Dad, I've decided what I'm going to do my project on, when my class goes to the agricultural show."

"Now, let me guess," laughed her father. "Would it be Jenny and Tilly, by any chance?"

Mandy nodded. "I bet James will want to write about them too," she said.

"Let's hope that Jenny wins again this year, then," said her dad. "Then you'll certainly have plenty to write about!"

"I hope so," Mandy agreed. "Isn't Tilly gorgeous?"

"Yes, she is," replied Mr Hope. "I expect Mike and Rachel are very pleased with her."

Mandy remembered what Mike had been talking about when they'd had tea.

"Do you look after Mike's brother's cow too?" she asked.

Her father shook his head. "No, Rob Talbot goes to the vet in Walton."

"Oh." Mandy wondered what Rob Talbot's Dexter cow was like. If he was entering his cow in the Rare Breeds class, Mandy would be able to see her at the show. "Do you know what Rob Talbot's cow is called?"

"Buttercup, I believe," Mr Hope replied, as they drove out of the farmyard.

"That's a good name for a cow," Mandy said.

"But not quite as good as Tilly!" her dad teased.

Mandy grinned. "Buttercup and her calf will have to be *really* beautiful to beat Jenny and Tilly."

"Well, Buttercup hasn't beaten Jenny yet." Mr Hope turned on to the main road. "We'll have to see what happens at the show. Rob and Mike are very good farmers but unfortunately they don't get on all that well."

"Why not?" Mandy asked.

"Rob's farm is right next door to Mike's," her dad explained. "It used to be one big family farm, but Rob wanted his own land, so they split it in half. Mike wasn't very happy about it."

"Oh." Mandy looked out of the window, at the green countryside rolling past. The poster for the show flashed past in a bright yellow blur, and Mandy began to feel excited. Tilly was truly the most beautiful calf that she had ever seen. Mandy was *sure* that Tilly and her mum would win the Rare Breeds class at the show!

3

Tilly's first lesson

Mandy looked up at the clock on the classroom wall. It felt like she'd been looking at it all day. Why did the hours always tick away so *slowly* when you were waiting for something exciting to happen?

"Time to tidy up, everyone," called Mrs Todd, Mandy's teacher. "And be quick, please. I want to speak to you before the bell rings."

Mandy jumped up from her chair and went to put her books away. Today, her mum was coming to collect Mandy and James from school and take them over to Treetop Farm. James was going to meet Tilly for the first time!

Mrs Todd looked around the room, waiting for everyone to sit down quietly. "Now," she began, "it's about our class visit to the agricultural show next week. I'm still waiting for some of you to bring the forms back. Your parents must sign the form or you won't be allowed to go. And that would be a shame, because it's going to be a lovely day."

Mandy grinned to herself. She'd brought her form back the day after it was given out!

"We must have all the forms back by the end of this week," Mrs Todd went on, as the bell rang. "Now, off you go."

Mandy was first on her feet. She grabbed her bag and hurried out of the classroom. She'd been so quick that James probably wouldn't be outside yet. He was in Mrs Black's class, the year below Mandy's.

"Wait for me, Mandy!" puffed a voice in her ear.

Mandy spun round, and there was James, grinning at her. "You were quick," she laughed.

"Not as quick as you!" replied James, pushing his glasses up his nose. "Come on. Let's go and see if your mum's here."

Mandy and James ran out into the playground, just as Mrs Hope drew up at the kerb in the Land-rover. They raced over to the car and jumped in.

"Hello, you two," said Emily Hope with a smile. "I don't think I've ever seen you move so fast!"

"We can't wait to see Tilly, Mum," Mandy said breathlessly. "I've told James all about her."

"I'm looking forward to seeing Tilly myself." Mrs Hope pulled carefully away from the kerb. "Your dad tells me she's lovely."

"Oh, she is," Mandy agreed. "And so is Jenny."

Mrs Hope drove out into the countryside towards Treetop Farm. Once again, it was a scorchingly hot day. It was almost *too* hot, Mandy decided. She hoped that the weather would stay fine for the show, but cool off a bit so that the animals weren't uncomfortable.

Rachel Talbot was out in the farmyard

feeding the hens when they drove through the gates. She waved at them. "Hello, Emily," she said cheerfully. "Hello, Mandy. And this must be James?"

James grinned and nodded.

"How are Tilly and Jenny, Mrs Talbot?" Mandy asked.

"They're fine." Mrs Talbot beamed. "Doing very well. Come and have a look."

Mandy and James followed her across the yard to the barn.

"Mike's out in the fields a lot at the moment," Mrs Talbot explained, pushing open the heavy door, "so I've been keeping an eye on these two."

Jenny and her calf were in their pen. Two pairs of large, dark eyes looked at the visitors with interest.

"Oh!" James stopped beside the gate and stared at the calf. "You were right, Mandy. She's lovely!"

Tilly stepped daintily forward to look at them a bit more closely. Mandy could see that Tilly was much steadier on her feet now, and she seemed much more alert and interested in everything. Her small, round ears were pricked, and she lifted her furry teddy bear face to sniff Mandy through the bars.

"Hello, Tilly." Mandy gently scratched the calf's reddish-brown head. "Do you remember me?"

Tilly rubbed her damp nose against Mandy's fingers. Meanwhile, Jenny began to butt her head against the bars of the pen, trying to reach James's pockets.

"Jenny!" Mrs Talbot laughed. "I'm afraid

she's very greedy, James. She's looking to see if you've got any food."

"I've got some jelly beans," said James.

"Well, Jenny can smell food a mile off!" said Mrs Talbot. "But I don't think jelly beans are very good for her."

"No, they certainly aren't," Mandy's mum agreed with a smile.

James moved away from the pen, leaving Jenny looking disappointed.

"I'm going to start getting Jenny and Tilly ready for the show soon," said Mrs Talbot. "There's always quite a lot to do."

"Like what?" Mandy asked.

"Well, we wash our cows so that they look nice and smart," she replied. "And then we have to get Tilly used to walking round with her mum, like they do at the show. Jenny and Tilly have to wear headcollars, too." Mrs Talbot smiled. "A lot of calves don't like that at first. So I'll practise putting a headcollar on Tilly and leading her round."

"How long will Jenny and Tilly stay in the pen?" Mandy wondered.

"They'll be going out into the fields

tomorrow, for a few hours every day," Mrs Talbot replied, tickling Jenny between her horns. "But we'll bring them in at night."

"Could we visit Jenny and Tilly again, before the show?" Mandy asked shyly. "If you're not too busy."

Mrs Talbot smiled at her. "I've got a better idea," she said. "Why don't you and James help me groom Jenny and Tilly and get them ready for the show?"

Mandy and James looked at each other in delight. "Yes, please!" Mandy gasped.

"As long as you're sure they won't be in the way, Rachel," Mandy's mum added.

"Not at all," Mrs Talbot said firmly. "I'm sure they'll be a great help."

"Did you hear that, Tilly?" Mandy whispered, stroking the calf's nose. "We're going to make sure that you and your mum are the best-groomed cow and calf in the whole show!"

"Are Jenny and Tilly out in the field, Mrs Talbot?" Mandy asked, looking into the empty pen.

It was Friday, after school, and Mandy and

James had come over to Treetop Farm to help the farmer's wife with Jenny and Tilly for the first time. Mandy and James had talked about nothing else ever since their visit to the farm, and they couldn't wait to get started. But when they ran into the barn, there was no sign of the pretty cow and her calf.

Mrs Talbot nodded. "They're spending quite a lot of time outside," she said. "But as we're going to groom Jenny now, we'll go and get them from the field." She was carrying a metal scoop and a headcollar made of soft white rope. "Jenny's used to wearing one of these," said Mrs Talbot, showing Mandy and James the headcollar. "But I don't think we'll try it on Tilly just yet!"

"What's that?" Mandy asked, peering into the metal scoop. It was full of something brown and crumbly.

"They're cattle nuts," Rachel explained. "Jenny's favourite snack! She'll do anything for them."

They walked round to the back of the farmhouse. Beyond the garden, there was a small paddock where Jenny was grazing away contentedly, with Tilly standing close beside her, looking around.

"Jenny!" called Mrs Talbot, rattling the cattle nuts in the scoop. Jenny immediately looked up. She trotted over to the fence, with Tilly following her like a little brown shadow.

"She'll always come for something to eat," laughed Mrs Talbot, giving Jenny a few of the cattle nuts. "Good girl, Jenny. Now let's put your headcollar on."

Mandy and James stroked Tilly while Mrs Talbot fitted the headcollar on to Jenny.

"James, would you like to lead Jenny?" asked Mrs Talbot, holding out the lead rope. "And, Mandy, you could walk behind with Tilly, even though she isn't wearing a headcollar. That will get her used to walking beside someone."

"OK," Mandy agreed eagerly. James looked a bit nervous, but he nodded and took the lead rope.

"Just go at a nice, steady pace," Mrs Talbot told him. "Walk next to Jenny's shoulder, so that she leads you, rather than you dragging her along."

Mandy watched James lead Jenny out of the

field. Jenny walked calmly beside him, her hooves making a soft rubbery clopping sound on the cobbled yard. As soon as Jenny began to move, Tilly trotted after her with an anxious, high-pitched moo. Mandy had to walk quite quickly to keep up with the little calf. She stroked her back from time to time, to remind Tilly there was someone beside her.

When they reached the farmyard, Mrs Talbot tied Jenny up outside the barn. Tilly stopped too, right behind her mum.

"Well done!" said Rachel with a smile. She went into the barn, and came out with some brushes. She gave one to James and one to Mandy. "These are stiff brushes to get the mud off," she explained. "After that, we use a softer brush to give the coat a lovely shine, and then we finish off with a cloth."

Mandy and James set to work, brushing Jenny's smooth red hair. Jenny didn't seem to mind at all. She stood patiently while Mandy and James cleaned every speck of mud and dirt from her coat. Tilly watched curiously and gently headbutted Mandy and James's legs every so often, as if she wanted to join in.

"Tilly wants to look as clean as her mum!" Mandy laughed. So, while James brushed Jenny's coat to a lovely, sleek shine, Mandy began to groom Tilly. The calf was too young to be tied up like Jenny, so Mrs Talbot held her firmly while Mandy brushed her. Tilly wasn't sure if she liked it at first, and she wriggled a bit, but she soon relaxed, and even closed her eyes as if she was going to sleep. Soon, Jenny and Tilly both had shiny, smooth, clean coats.

"What about their tails?" asked James. "They're a bit mucky."

"Oh, can we wash them?" Mandy said eagerly.

"Well, we wouldn't usually clean their tails until the day before the show," Mrs Talbot explained. "But I don't suppose it will hurt to give them an extra wash!" She disappeared into the farmhouse, and came out carrying a bucket of warm water. She poured in a capful of cow shampoo and swished the water with her hand until the bucket was full of frothy white bubbles. Then she held the bucket beside Jenny and dipped the tail into the soapy water, swooshing it around.

"Just like washing a pair of socks!" laughed James.

"Do you know how to dry a cow's tail?" Mrs Talbot asked when she had rinsed Jenny's tail in a bucket of clean water.

Mandy and James looked puzzled.

"With a towel?" suggested James.

Rachel shook her head. "Stand clear!" she warned them. She picked up Jenny's tail and began to spin it around in a circle, very fast. Drops of water flew everywhere.

Mandy and James burst out laughing.

"Tilly looks amazed, doesn't she?" James pointed out. The little calf was staring at her mum's tail whizzing round as if she couldn't believe her eyes.

"Your turn next, Tilly!" said Mrs Talbot. "Mandy, would you like to clean Tilly's tail? It's OK, you don't have to spin it round to dry it," she added with a smile. "A calf's tail is much less hairy than a cow's, so we'll just dry Tilly off with a towel."

So Mandy fetched another bucket of water and washed Tilly's tail, and patted it dry. Soon the calf's tail was soft and white, just like her mum's.

"Well done, Tilly!" said Mandy, putting her arms round the calf's neck and hugging her.

"It's a shame there's not a class for the cleanest tails," joked James. "Jenny and Tilly would win it easily!"

"Here's your dad, Mandy," said Mrs Talbot, as the Hopes' Land-rover pulled into the farmyard.

"Oh, is it time for us to go already?" Mandy said, feeling a bit disappointed.

Mr Hope climbed out of the Land-rover. He had a newspaper in his hand, and he waved it at them. "Guess who's in the *Walton Gazette* today?" he called with a smile.

"It must be the picture of Jenny and Tilly!" Mandy exclaimed, and ran towards him. "Dad, can we see?"

Mr Hope handed over the newspaper, and Mandy and James flicked through it until they came to the right page. There was a large photo of Jenny and Tilly, with Mandy stroking the calf, and a short article underneath.

"What a lovely picture," said Mrs Talbot, who was looking over Mandy and James's shoulders.

"Don't Jenny and Tilly look great?" Mandy said happily. "Dad, can I cut the picture out and keep it?"

"Of course," Mr Hope agreed, his eyes twinkling. "But *after* I've read the newspaper!"

"Maybe Jenny and Tilly will be in the *Walton Gazette* again," James pointed out. "If they win a prize at the show."

"I hope so," Mandy said eagerly.

Mandy opened her eyes and yawned. It was Saturday morning, and she'd been dreaming about the agricultural show. Jenny and Tilly had won all the prizes! It had been a lovely dream, but something had woken her up . . .

It was the telephone, ringing in the hall downstairs. Mandy sat up in bed and looked at her clock. It was only half-past seven. It must be an animal emergency, she thought drowsily. If Animal Ark was closed, people could ring the Hopes' own number instead.

Mandy climbed out of bed, and went over to the top of the stairs. She could hear her mum talking to someone.

"I'll be there as soon as I can, Mike," Emily

Hope was saying. "And don't worry, Tilly will be fine."

Tilly? Mandy's heart began to thump.

"Mum!" She ran down the stairs. "What's wrong? What's happened to Tilly?"

"It's not Tilly, love," said her mum, putting the receiver down. She looked very worried. "It's Jenny. I'm afraid she's disappeared."

4

Where is Jenny?

"Oh!" Mandy stared at her mum in horror.
"Did Jenny escape from the barn?"

"It looks that way," Mrs Hope replied. "They
were in the pen last night, as usual. But this
morning Jenny wasn't there."

Mandy bit her lip. This was awful. "Jenny
wouldn't leave Tilly, Mum," she said in a wobbly
voice. "I know she wouldn't. Is Tilly OK?"

Mrs Hope put her arm round Mandy. "Mike wants me to go up there and check her over," she said. "He can feed her on powdered milk while Jenny's missing, so Tilly will be all right. But Mike sounds pretty upset."

"Can I come?" Mandy asked quickly. "And James too?"

Mrs Hope frowned. "I'm not sure that's a good idea," she began.

"Oh, *please*, Mum," Mandy begged. "We won't get in the way, and we could help look for Jenny."

"Well, I'll ring Mike back and ask him if that's all right," said her mum. "You run upstairs and get dressed."

Mandy hurried up to her bedroom. She was so worried, she was all fingers and thumbs as she pulled on her sweatshirt and jeans. Where was Jenny?

"Mike says it's fine," called Mrs Hope, as Mandy ran downstairs again. "You and James can come with me."

"Oh, good." Mandy felt very relieved. Quickly she picked up the phone and dialled James's number.

"Hello?" It was James's voice.

"Oh, sorry, James. Did I wake you up?" Mandy said anxiously. She was so worried about Jenny, she'd forgotten how early it was.

"No, it's OK. Blackie woke me up at half past six," James said grumpily. Blackie was James's Labrador puppy. "He was barking at a blackbird!"

"Oh, James, you'll never guess what's happened," Mandy burst out. "Jenny's disappeared."

"What!" James sounded horrified, and much more awake.

Quickly Mandy explained what had happened. "Mum and I are going over to the farm now," she finished. "Do you want to come too? We can look for Jenny."

"Of course I will," said James. "Poor Jenny!"

Soon, Mandy and her mum were heading over to the Hunters' house.

James was watching for them. He came running out, his face solemn. "Is there any news?" he asked, as he climbed into the Land-rover.

Mandy shook her head. No one said anything

more as Mrs Hope drove towards Treetop Farm. When they arrived, Mrs Talbot came out of the barn to meet them. Mandy could tell from the look on her face that Jenny hadn't come back.

"Mike's searched the outbuildings, and now he's looking round the fields," Rachel explained. "But there's no sign of Jenny so far."

"How did Jenny get out of her pen?" asked James.

Rachel shook her head, looking puzzled. "We're not quite sure," she replied. "The latch on the gate is a bit loose. If Jenny had nudged it with her nose, she could have opened it, I suppose."

"How's Tilly?" Mandy asked anxiously.

"I've just been feeding her," said Mrs Talbot. "She's all right, but she's missing her mum."

Mandy felt very sorry for the little calf.

"I just hope we find Jenny soon," Mrs Talbot went on, looking even more worried. "It could be dangerous for her if she's not being milked."

Mandy glanced at James. They both knew that cows had to be milked regularly, or their udders would swell up and get infected. Things were going from bad to worse.

They all went into the barn so that Mrs Talbot could finish feeding Tilly. She held up a bucket of warm milk, and Tilly stuck her head in to suck up the last drops. Mandy was glad to see that at least Tilly was feeding properly, even though her mum wasn't there. But as soon as the milk was finished, Tilly began pacing round and round the pen, mooing loudly and looking miserable.

"She's not used to being on her own," said Mrs Talbot.

"Poor Tilly," Mandy said sadly. She looked more closely at the latch on the gate. It *did* look rather loose, although she hadn't noticed it before.

Just then Mike hurried into the barn. He looked tired and pale, and very concerned. "I've searched all the farm buildings and the fields," he said grimly. "I can't find Jenny anywhere."

Mandy's heart sank. "Where *can* she be?" she asked in a wobbly voice.

"If she's not on our land, then she must have wandered on to the moors," Mike replied, his face serious.

Mandy gasped in horror, and looked at James. The moors stretched for miles around the farm in all directions. Jenny could be *anywhere*.

"We'd better start searching right away," said Mrs Talbot, sounding very determined.

"Can James and I help?" Mandy asked eagerly.

"If your mum doesn't mind." Mike raised his eyebrows at Mrs Hope, who nodded and smiled at Mandy.

"Actually, Emily, I've got a couple of other cows calving at the moment," Mike went on. "I'd be really grateful if you could take a quick look at them, now that you're here."

"Of course," said Mrs Hope, and she and Mike left the barn. Meanwhile, Mrs Talbot went over to a large sack in the corner.

"We'll take some cattle nuts with us," she said to Mandy and James. "The noise of the nuts rattling in the scoop might attract Jenny's attention if she's close by."

Mandy's heart was thumping hard as Mrs Talbot led them through the farmyard and the fields, and out on to the moors. They *had* to find Jenny. They simply had to. Surely the little cow couldn't be very far away?

They began to walk slowly away from the farm, Mrs Talbot rattling the cattle nuts in the metal scoop. Mandy gazed round at the rolling green hills and valleys, hoping to spot Jenny hurrying towards them. But the pretty cow was nowhere to be seen.

"Oh, Jenny, where *are* you?" Mandy whispered, biting her lip. She couldn't bear to think of Jenny lost and alone and hungry, and missing Tilly.

They walked on, looking in each of the Talbots' fields. The sun was blazing in the blue sky, but Mandy was too busy to enjoy the beautiful day. Her heart began to sink as she realised they'd been searching for almost an hour now, and there was still no sign of Jenny.

"There's Mike and Mrs Hope," said James, pointing to two figures climbing over a gate on the other side of the field.

"We've searched on the other side of the farm," Mike announced wearily. "No Jenny, I'm afraid."

"We've had no luck either," sighed his wife. "It's as if Jenny's vanished into thin air."

Mandy felt a lump come into her throat as she thought about Tilly all alone in the pen without her mum.

"I'm going to take the truck out and drive

around the lanes for a while," Mike went on. "I can cover a much bigger area that way."

"I'll ring some of our neighbours," Mrs Talbot decided. "I'll ask them if they've seen Jenny."

"We've got to go, I'm afraid," said Mrs Hope, looking at her watch. "Good luck. I really hope Jenny turns up very soon."

"Maybe Mandy and I could come back tomorrow to help you look again," James offered.

"And if Jenny comes home, will you ring and tell us?" Mandy asked.

Mrs Talbot nodded. But Mandy could see that she and Mike didn't look very hopeful. Mandy couldn't help feeling miserable too. It was all such a mystery.

Where was Jenny?

"Mandy, I won't be able to take you and James to Treetop Farm until later," said Mrs Hope, picking up her bag. It was the following morning. Mandy had been hoping for a phone call from the Talbots to say that Jenny had returned, but they hadn't rung. That meant Jenny had been missing for a whole day and a night.

Mandy was very disappointed. "Oh, why not, Mum?"

"I have to go over to see a sick sheep at Redwood Farm," her mum explained. "I don't know how long I'll be there. I'll drop you off at Lilac Cottage on my way." Mandy's grandparents lived at Lilac Cottage in Welford, and she often stayed with them when her parents were busy. Mr Hope had gone to

York to see an old friend of his, who was also a vet.

"OK," Mandy agreed. "I'd better ring James because he'll be waiting for us to pick him up."

Mandy lifted the receiver, but as she did so, she heard a familiar bark outside the front door. She opened it and Blackie launched himself at her, barking a loud greeting and pulling James along behind him.

"Hello, Blackie!" Mandy laughed, fondling the puppy's silky ears. "What're you two doing here?"

"I decided to walk over," James panted. He looked out of breath. "Blackie needed some exercise, and I thought maybe he could help us look for Jenny."

"Well, maybe," Mandy said with a smile. Secretly she thought that Blackie would get in the way, rather than help! He was very sweet, but he was also very naughty.

James caught Mandy's eye and laughed. "OK, so he won't help very much!" he said. "But he could do with a really long walk."

"We can't go yet, anyway." Mandy explained

that her mum was just about to go on an emergency call to Redwood Farm.

James's eyes lit up behind his glasses. "Redwood Farm?" he echoed. "That's not far from the Talbots'. If your mum dropped us off there, we could have another look for Jenny."

"That's a great idea, James," Mandy agreed. She ran off to ask her mum.

"Well, all right," said Mrs Hope. "But you're to stay in sight of the farm buildings. Is that clear?"

Mandy and James nodded.

Mandy began to feel quite hopeful again as her mum drove them through the countryside towards Redwood Farm. At least they were *doing* something by looking for Jenny. Mandy wondered how Tilly was. She hoped the little calf wasn't too miserable.

Emily Hope stopped at the gates of Redwood Farm to let them out of the car. "Now remember what I said," she warned them. "Don't go wandering off over the moors. I don't want to lose you, too!"

Mandy and James waved, and set off across the fields. Blackie pulled at his lead and barked loudly whenever he spotted a bird overhead.

"Shall I let him off the lead?" James asked doubtfully.

Mandy shook her head. "We'd never catch him again," she said.

Suddenly Blackie stopped and sniffed the ground. He lunged forward, pulling James with him, and began to bark at a large clump of bushes.

"What is it, boy?" James asked eagerly.

"It's probably a rabbit," Mandy said.

Blackie crawled on his tummy into the bushes, and then reappeared looking very proud of himself, his tail wagging madly. He had an empty crisp packet in his mouth.

James looked a bit disappointed. "Blackie, put that down!" he scolded, trying to pull the crisp packet away from the puppy.

They walked on a bit further, calling Jenny's name as they went. As Mandy had suspected, Blackie wasn't very helpful. He kept trying to run off every time he spotted a rabbit, so James kept him on a tight lead.

"We'll have to go back." Mandy turned and looked over her shoulder. They'd gone a little further than they were supposed to along a moorland track, and the farm buildings were just out of sight. "Mum might be waiting for us." She looked down at Blackie, who was whining softly at their feet. "What's the matter, boy? Have you seen another rabbit?"

Blackie gave a loud bark and began jumping around James's legs. His ears were twitching and his tail wagged so fast, it was a black blur. He seemed to be trying to drag James towards a tumbledown stone hut a few metres away.

"No, Blackie!" James said sternly. "No more crisp packets and no more rabbits for you. We're going home."

Mandy glanced over at the hut. She knew farmers and walkers used it as a shelter when they were caught out on the moors in bad weather. She was just about to turn away when she heard a muffled noise.

"What's that?" she said to James.

They waited and listened. There was another noise, louder this time. *Moooo!*

"James!" Mandy cried. "Did you hear that?"

James was already rushing over to the hut, with Blackie racing along in front of him.

Mandy caught them up just as James reached for the door handle. The door was rather stiff, and they both had to push hard to get it open.

Another loud moo greeted them as they rushed in.

And there, inside the hut, was Jenny!

5

Safe and sound

"Jenny!" Mandy gasped with relief. "How did you get in here?"

Jenny mooed loudly. She seemed very pleased to see them. Mandy and James ran over to her and the little cow butted her head gently against their chests. She seemed fine, except that she was quite dirty, covered in mud and cobwebs. Someone had left her a pile of hay and a bucket of water on the floor. She was standing in a deep bed of clean straw, and more straw bales were stacked in one corner.

"She looks all right, doesn't she?" James sounded just as relieved as Mandy. "I wonder if she's been milked?"

Mandy glanced at Jenny's udder. It looked round, but not too swollen. "I think someone *has* milked her," she said. She pointed at the bucket of water. "Someone's obviously been looking after her. But we'd better get Mike here as fast as we can."

"What shall we do now?" asked James. "Shall I run and tell your mum?"

Mandy nodded. "That's a good idea," she said. "She'll be able to phone Mike. I'll wait here with Jenny."

James nodded, and he and Blackie disappeared outside. Mandy went to the door and watched them race towards the farm. Then she went back to Jenny and put her arm round the cow's neck. "Poor Jenny," she said softly. "Have you missed your baby?"

Mandy ran her hands gently over Jenny's back, brushing away the cobwebs. Some of

them were very sticky, and would need to be removed with a stiff brush. Her coat was no longer smooth and clean, and there were only a few days before the show! Still, at least they'd found Jenny, Mandy thought, and she was safe. That was the most important thing.

Mandy glanced round the hut and shivered. It was quite gloomy and dirty. She hoped Jenny hadn't been too frightened all on her own. "Don't worry, Jenny," Mandy whispered in the cow's big velvety ear. "You'll soon be home with Tilly."

It seemed like a long time before Mandy heard voices outside the hut. She ran over to the door. Her mum, James and Blackie were hurrying towards the hut. Mrs Hope had her vet's bag with her.

"Well done, love," Mrs Hope said to Mandy, as they came into the hut. "Mike and Rachel are really thrilled. I've phoned them, and Mike's on his way."

"I *think* Jenny's OK," Mandy said anxiously. "But I'm not sure."

"We'll soon find out," her mum replied. She took out her stethoscope and began to listen to

Jenny's breathing, while Mandy and James watched closely.

Before Mrs Hope had finished checking Jenny over, however, there were footsteps outside. A moment later, Mike stood in the doorway, breathing hard. He had a headcollar in his hand. "I left the truck down at Redwood Farm and ran up here!" he panted. "Hello, Jenny! It's good to see you again, girl."

Jenny mooed, then licked Mike's hand.

"Is she OK?" he asked Emily Hope. "She's been milked, I can see that."

"She seems fine," Mandy's mum replied. "But let's get her home now, shall we? I can finish checking her over at the farm."

"Good idea." Mike slipped the headcollar around Jenny's neck. "I wonder how she found her way in here?"

"Maybe the door was open and she just wandered in," Mandy suggested. "Then she got stuck, because the door closed somehow. It's really hard to open."

"But someone's been looking after her," said James, pointing to the bucket of water. "So somebody knew she was in here."

Mandy and James walked towards the pen, but before they got close enough to read the label on the front, they heard a loud voice behind them.

"I'm telling you, I want to make a complaint!"

Mandy looked round. A man with a thick brown beard was pushing his way through the crowd in the tent, talking angrily to one of the stewards.

"The pen for my cow and her calf is far too small!" the man said furiously. "Come here, and I'll show you." He marched over to the pen, pushing past Mandy and James. He glared at them. "Would you please keep away from my animals?" he snapped. "I don't want them upset before the class."

Mandy and James moved away as fast as they could, and went back to Jenny and Tilly.

"He doesn't seem very happy," Mandy whispered.

"We weren't upsetting the animals," James added indignantly. "If anyone's upsetting them, it's *him* with his loud voice!"

The man was still complaining, while the steward listened patiently.

Mrs Hope frowned. "It seems a strange thing to do," she said. "If someone was worried that Jenny was lost and needed looking after, why didn't they try to find her owner?"

"Maybe they did, and they couldn't," Mandy suggested.

"So they decided to keep her in the shed, where she was safe," James added.

Mike shrugged. "Could be. Well, it's a bit of a mystery, but the main thing is that we've found her!" he said. "Come on, girl." He led Jenny over to the door. "Time to take you home to Tilly."

Mandy, James and Mrs Hope followed them out of the hut. Although Mandy was really relieved that Jenny was safe, she still couldn't help wondering what had happened. Mike was right, it *was* a mystery.

"You two can ride in the truck with me if you like," Mike suggested to Mandy and James when they reached Redwood Farm.

"Is that OK, Mum?" Mandy asked.

Mrs Hope nodded. "I'll follow you in the Land-rover," she said. "I've finished here."

Mike led Jenny into the trailer that was

attached to the back of his truck. Then he, Mandy and James climbed into the cab, and they drove off.

"I can't tell you how grateful I am to you two," Mike said cheerfully as they headed back to Treetop Farm. "Rachel and I were really worried."

"Jenny seems OK, though," Mandy said. "She was lucky that someone found her and looked after her."

"That's true," Mike agreed. "And now we can concentrate on the show."

When they pulled into the farmyard, Rachel Talbot came out of the barn, leading Tilly with her headcollar on.

Mandy leaned out of the window and waved. "Look, Tilly," she called. "We've brought your mum home!"

Tilly's big brown eyes looked anxious as she watched the truck and trailer pull into the yard. Mike jumped out and opened the trailer. He led Jenny out, and she gave a loud moo when she spotted her calf, tugging the leadrope right out of Mike's hands. Mandy and James watched as Jenny and Tilly rubbed their heads together.

Tilly stood very close to Jenny, pressed close against her side, as if she couldn't quite believe that her mum was home. Mandy smiled happily at the sight.

"Oh, Jenny, it's so good to see you!" said Mrs Talbot, beaming. "But you're very dirty. You'll need a good grooming before the show. We'll let you get used to being back home first, and save that for another day."

"Jenny seems fine," said Mrs Hope, climbing

out of her car. "But I should finish checking her over."

"We'll take Jenny and Tilly into the barn," said Mike, reaching for Tilly's lead rope.

"Good idea," said Mrs Talbot. "And I'll go and make us all a cup of tea. Mandy and James, why don't you come with me and tell me exactly how you found Tilly?"

Mandy and James followed Mrs Talbot into the kitchen, and while she put the kettle on, they told her all about finding Jenny in the hut.

Mrs Talbot looked quite upset. "Poor thing," she said. "Still, at least someone looked after her. And Jenny's safely home now, so there's no harm done."

At that moment, Mike and Mrs Hope came in.

"I think Tilly's making up for lost time," Mandy's mum said, smiling. "She was still tucking in when we left."

"And Jenny's not lost her appetite, either," said Mike. "She's eaten a whole scoop of nuts and half a bale of hay already!"

Mandy and James cheered. Jenny must be OK!

"And I've mended the loose latch on the gate of the pen," Mike added. "So all we've got to do now is think about the show."

Mandy nodded. She'd been so worried about Jenny, she'd almost forgotten about the show. But once Jenny had been washed and groomed again, she would be fine. And the show was next week! Mandy began to feel excited all over again. She couldn't wait.

6

Show time!

"Right, where is my Rare Breeds group?" called Mrs Todd, glancing at her clipboard.

Mandy's hand shot up. So did James's. It was the day of the school visit to the agricultural show, and the three classes that were going had gathered in the playground, along with their teachers and the parents who'd volunteered to help. The classes were being divided into groups, depending on which part of the show they were most interested in. Mandy and James had chosen Rare Breeds so that they could write about Jenny and Tilly.

"Come over here, please," said Mrs Todd, ticking the names off on her list. "Right, that's us sorted out, so I think we're ready to go."

Everyone cheered. Mrs Black and her Rural Crafts group led the way out into the street, and the others followed in a neat line. The show was held in a large park just outside Welford, not far from James's house, so it wasn't far to walk.

"The Talbots and Jenny and Tilly must be at the show by now," Mandy said, as she walked along next to James. "I bet they're all feeling excited."

"I hope Jenny isn't upset after getting lost like that," remarked James. "It might mean she doesn't do as well at the show this year."

"Well, the other cows would be pleased, because it would give them more of a chance!" Mandy said. "Especially Buttercup."

James looked puzzled. "Who's Buttercup?"

"Rob Talbot's Dexter cow," Mandy

reminded him. "You know, Mike's brother."

James nodded. "Oh, yes."

The crocodile of pupils snaked its way past James's house.

Mandy nudged him. "There's Blackie in the front garden with your mum," she said with a grin.

Mrs Hunter was weeding the garden, but every time she pulled up a weed Blackie tried

to grab it and run off with it. The people at the head of the line started laughing.

Mrs Hunter heard the laughter, turned round and waved. "Are you sure you wouldn't like to take Blackie with you?" she called with a smile. Meanwhile, Blackie had spotted James and Mandy. He dashed over to the gate and began to bark loudly.

"No thanks, Mum!" said James, giving Blackie a quick pat through the bars of the gate.

The show had just started by the time the classes from Welford Primary arrived. It was a lovely, sunny day, and there were already queues of people at the gates. But there was a special schools entrance, and in no time at all they were inside.

Mandy looked around eagerly. There was so much going on! There were large show-rings at one end of the park, and huge tents dotted around them, which housed the animals. There were lots of stalls selling flowers, fruit, vegetables and all sorts of home-made food. In one display ring, two men were showing the audience how to build a drystone wall, and next to that was a stall selling corn dollies. In front of the stall, a group of women sat at a table, giving a demonstration of how corn dollies were made.

"We'll all meet up again at the schools tent for lunch at one o'clock sharp," said Mrs Todd. The other groups began to gather round the grown-ups who were in charge of them, ready to start work on their special projects.

"Let's go and find the Rare Breeds tents," Mrs Todd went on, smiling at her small group.

"I think they're over there," said James, pointing to a sign.

There were several different tents for the rare breeds, but to Mandy and James's delight, Mrs Todd said that they could go and see the cows first.

"Mandy has been telling us all about Jenny and Tilly in class," she said with a smile, "so I think it would be a good idea to go and have a look at them. They're Dexter cows, aren't they, Mandy?"

Mandy nodded. "Yes, they are."

"Now, remember," Mrs Todd went on, as she led the group towards the tent, "make sure you take lots of notes about what the cows look like, and perhaps make some sketches too."

Everyone in the group had a clipboard and a pencil, and several sheets of plain paper. Mandy's heart was thumping with excitement as they went into the tent. She was really looking forward to seeing Jenny and Tilly.

"Look, Mandy." James nudged her. "See the Highland cattle over there?"

With their long, shaggy, red coats and huge horns, the Highland cattle were getting a lot of attention. There was already a large crowd round their pens.

"Let's find Jenny and Tilly first," Mandy suggested. "We can start making our notes after that."

James nodded, and they began to weave their way through the people in the tent, looking for the Dexter cows. Mandy couldn't help stopping to look at some cows she'd never seen before. They looked like giant teddy bears with their huge round heads, thick black coats, and a wide white stripe going all the way round their middle.

"They're Belted Galloways," said James, reading the name off the sign nearby. "Aren't they great, Mandy?"

"And that white stripe looks *just* like a belt," Mandy laughed.

The Dexter cows were right at the other end of the tent, in a row of six pens. Each pen held a cow with her calf. There was no sign of Mike Talbot, but Mandy spotted Jenny and Tilly immediately. "There they are!" she said to James.

They rushed over to the pen, which was labelled *Treetop Jenny and Treetop Tilly*. Jenny gave a moo of delight, and pushed her nose against Mandy's hand as she leaned into the pen to stroke her. Jenny looked beautifully clean again. Her chestnut coat gleamed like a newly-polished conker. And Tilly, who was butting her head against James's fingers, also looked lovely with her soft, wavy coat and big, dark eyes.

James glanced round at the other Dexter cows and calves. "I think Jenny and Tilly are the best, Mandy," he whispered.

Mandy grinned. "They look lovely, too," she said, pointing at the cow and calf in the pen opposite. The cow was brown, like Jenny, and the pretty little calf was black.

"Let's go over and see what their names are," suggested James.

"All the pens are exactly the same size, Mr Talbot," said the steward when he could finally get a word in.

"Mr Talbot!" Mandy gasped, clutching James's arm. "You know who that is, don't you, James? It's Mike's brother!"

7

What's going on?

"So that must be Buttercup," said James in a low voice.

The steward had just about managed to calm Rob Talbot down, although he was still looking angry and muttering under his breath. People had begun to stare, and Buttercup and her calf shifted restlessly in their pen.

Mandy watched as Rob Talbot carried on

talking to the steward, but in a lower voice. Then the steward turned and walked off, but Rob Talbot still didn't look very happy. At that moment, Mike appeared and came towards Mandy and James.

"Ah, hello, Mike," called Rob Talbot in a booming voice. "Jenny and Tilly are looking very well."

Mandy could see that he was trying to be friendly, but somehow it didn't quite work. He didn't really *sound* friendly.

"Thank you, Rob," replied Mike, looking a bit uncomfortable. He turned to Mandy and James and smiled. "Hello, you two."

"Where's Mrs Talbot?" asked James.

"She's helping out on one of the stalls," Mike explained. "But she'll be finished in time for the class. I'm going to lead Jenny, and she'll take Tilly."

"We'll be cheering really loudly for you!" James told him.

"That's great," Mike said cheerfully. Then he glanced over at the pen opposite. "That's my brother's cow, Buttercup, and her calf, Tansy," he said, his smile fading.

Mandy and James looked at each other. They didn't like to say that they'd already met Mike's brother, and thought he was very rude.

"How's your project going?" Mike asked, peering down at their clipboards. "Have you done much yet?"

"We haven't even started!" Mandy said. She'd almost forgotten they were supposed to be making notes about the animals. "We'd better get to work, James."

"OK. Why don't we start right here with Jenny and Tilly?" suggested James.

"Don't forget, the class begins at 2 o'clock," Mike reminded them. "If you come back here a bit earlier, you can help me give Jenny and Tilly a final polish."

"We'd love to!" Mandy said, her eyes shining. "But we'll have to ask Mrs Todd first."

"Well, hopefully I'll see you then," grinned Mike. Then he went over to talk to another farmer, who was standing by one of the Belted Galloway pens.

"I don't think Mike likes his brother much," James said thoughtfully, as he and Mandy put a clean piece of paper on the top of their clipboards.

"Well, my dad says they don't really get on," Mandy replied. "Look, James, Tilly's having a drink from Jenny. I'm going to draw her like that." She rested her clipboard on the top rail of the pen and began to draw an outline of the calf.

When they had finished their pictures, they said goodbye to Jenny and Tilly and walked slowly round the other pens, noting down all the different breeds of cows and what they looked like. Then Mrs Todd gathered everyone together, and they went into some of the other Rare Breeds tents. Mandy and James really liked the Gloucestershire Old Spot pigs, with their drooping ears and sleepy, beady eyes. There was so much to see, and so many things to write down, that soon they both had pages of notes and sketches.

"These chickens are massive!" James said to Mandy. They were looking at a pen of Black Jersey Giants, huge black hens with bright pink crests. "I think they would even scare Blackie!"

Mrs Todd appeared beside them. "We're going over to the schools' tent now," she said. "It's time for lunch."

"Mrs Todd, Mike Talbot asked if James and I could help him to groom Jenny and Tilly before the show," Mandy said. "So would it be all right if we ate our lunch there? Then we can get on with the grooming as soon as we've finished."

"I don't see why not," said Mrs Todd. Mandy and James looked at each other in delight. "As long as it's all right with Mr Talbot. You can meet us all at the show-ring when the class begins."

"Thank you, Mrs Todd," Mandy said.

The teacher's eyes twinkled. "And I expect to see some really excellent work from you about Jenny and Tilly tomorrow!" She turned to the rest of the group. "Let's go then. I'm sure you're hungry after all your hard work!"

Mrs Todd and the others went off, and Mandy and James made their way back to the tent where the cows were being kept. As they got nearer, Mike came out. He had a bucket in his hand. "Hello, you two," he said with a grin. "I hope you've told your teacher where you are. I don't want to get you into trouble!"

"Mrs Todd said we could eat our lunch here with you," Mandy explained. "And then we can help you groom Jenny and Tilly."

"That sounds like a good idea," said Mike. "I'm just going to collect the grooming kit from the truck."

"What's the bucket for?" asked James.

"Tilly's tail could do with another wash," Mike said. "I thought maybe the refreshments tent could give me some warm water."

"We could get that before we have our lunch," James offered.

"Thanks." Mike handed the bucket to James. "I'll see you in a few minutes then."

Mike went off, and Mandy turned to James. "Do you know where the refreshments tent is?"

"I think I saw it over there." James pointed across the field. Mandy looked in the direction he was pointing and saw Rob Talbot standing near one of the tents. To her surprise, she saw him duck out of sight behind the tent when he spotted Mike walking across the grass.

"That's funny," Mandy said, puzzled.

"What is?" asked James.

Mandy told him what she'd seen.

"Maybe Rob Talbot just didn't want to talk to his brother," James suggested. Mandy nodded, but then she saw Rob Talbot pop out from behind the tent again. He looked quickly from side to side, as if he was checking that Mike had gone, then he turned and hurried off in the opposite direction.

Rob Talbot seemed to be heading for the refreshments tent too, so Mandy and James were not far behind him. He looked very nervous. He kept on wiping his brow with his handkerchief, and glancing around as if he was waiting for someone.

"Look, James," Mandy said in a low voice. "Don't you think he's acting a bit funny?"

"Maybe he's just worried about losing to Jenny again," replied James.

Suddenly Mandy spotted a boy of about thirteen making his way towards Rob Talbot. The boy was tall and thin, with curly brown hair and a sulky look on his face. Rob grabbed

his arm as if he was afraid the boy was going to run off, and started speaking urgently to him. But Mandy and James were too far away to hear what they were saying.

"It looks like they're arguing," Mandy whispered to James. Rob Talbot was looking very annoyed, and wasn't letting the boy say much at all. Finally the boy nodded. Then Rob Talbot pulled a plastic bag out of his pocket and pressed it into the boy's hand. But, again, Mandy and James were too far away to see what was in the bag.

"That was a bit strange, don't you think?" Mandy asked, as Rob and the boy went off in different directions. "I wonder what's in that bag?"

James shrugged. "It's probably nothing much. Come on, let's go and get this water."

Mandy followed James towards the refreshments tent, but she couldn't help looking back over her shoulder at Rob Talbot. James was right, there could be lots of different things in that plastic bag. But somehow Mandy couldn't get it out of her mind.

8

Trouble in the ring

"Jenny!" Mandy protested with a laugh. "Stop trying to steal my sandwich!"

Jenny was leaning over the top of the pen, trying to grab it. Now she mooed loudly, and looked longingly at the sandwich in Mandy's hand.

"Jenny, you're a very greedy girl," Mike said sternly. He winked at Mandy and James. "She'll get an extra-special meal tonight if she wins the class again," he added.

A group of people was wandering around looking at the Dexter cows. They stopped beside Jenny and Tilly's pen, and stared at them admiringly.

"What a beautiful little calf!" exclaimed a woman wearing a flowery dress.

Mandy and James looked proudly at Tilly. The calf was looking up at the woman with her big, brown eyes, and she *did* look gorgeous.

"She's a beautiful little calf with a mucky tail!" Mike joked, as the lady moved away. "If you've finished your lunch, shall we get on with the grooming?" He glanced at his watch. "Rachel should be here in a minute."

Mandy and James put their lunchboxes away, and then joined Mike inside the pen. Jenny sniffed them eagerly, and even found a few sandwich crumbs on James's sleeve, which she licked off with her long pink tongue.

James and Mike began brushing Jenny, while Mandy gently washed Tilly's tail and dried it with an old towel. Tilly stood very still. She didn't seem bothered by all the people crowding round the pen. Mandy didn't think that Tilly would mind walking round the show-ring in front of a big audience either. She'd behave perfectly, Mandy was sure of that.

"Sorry I'm late!" Rachel Talbot rushed into the tent, looking a bit flustered. "The cake stall was so busy, I just couldn't get away. And then the woman taking over from me was late." She leaned into the pen and smiled at Mandy and James. "Jenny and Tilly look great!" she said warmly. "Thanks for all your hard work."

"Excuse me! Would you mind getting out of my way?"

Mandy had heard that loud voice before. She looked round, and there was Rob Talbot bustling his way through the crowd. He was carrying a bucket of water and a shallow plastic box of grooming brushes. People jumped aside to let him pass, and Rob let himself into Buttercup and Tansy's pen. He glanced over at Jenny and Tilly, and Rachel Talbot raised her hand and smiled at him. Rob Talbot nodded briskly at her, then turned his back and began to groom Buttercup. Mandy saw Mrs Talbot

raise her eyebrows at her husband, but neither of them said anything.

Mandy finished rubbing Tilly's coat all over with a soft cloth, then stood back to take a good look. Tilly's coat was now sleek, smooth and shiny. Mandy gave the calf a hug. "You look brilliant, Tilly," she whispered into her fluffy ear.

"Attention, please!" One of the stewards was speaking over the tannoy. "The Rare Breeds class will be starting in fifteen minutes' time. The first Cow and Calf class will be for Dexters."

"That's you two, Jenny," said James, scratching Jenny between her horns. Jenny mooed, as if to say *I'm ready*!

"We'd better go, James," Mandy said. "We have to meet up with Mrs Todd and the rest of our group."

"Good luck," James said to the Talbots.

"And don't forget to cheer us on!" Mike added. He was starting to look quite nervous too, although not as nervous as his brother. Mandy noticed that Rob Talbot had even knocked over the bucket of water he'd taken into the pen to clean Buttercup and Tansy, because he'd been fussing around so much.

Mike and Rachel fitted the headcollars on to Jenny and Tilly as Mandy and James slipped out of the pen.

"I feel nervous too!" Mandy confessed. She and James made their way out of the tent towards the show-ring. "I really want Jenny and Tilly to win."

"Me too," James agreed. "Look, there's Mrs Todd and the others. And they've got really good seats, close to the front."

"I hope they've saved us some!" Mandy said as they hurried towards the rest of their group.

"Hello," said a voice from behind them. "It's Mandy Hope, isn't it?"

Mandy looked round. Alison West, the reporter from the *Walton Gazette*, was smiling at her.

"Oh, hello!" Mandy said.

"I'm here to report on the show," Alison told her. "And, of course, I want to see if Jenny and Tilly win! Did you like the picture, by the way?"

Mandy nodded. "It was great."

"Well, I'd better go and get myself a good spot to take some photos!" Alison went on. "See you later."

She went off, and Mandy and James ran to join Mrs Todd and their group.

"Ah, here you are," said the teacher. "We've saved you some seats."

Mandy and James slipped into their seats at the end of the row, and waited impatiently for the class to begin. Mandy was so excited she could hardly sit still. She glanced round the audience. The rare breeds had attracted plenty of interest, and there were lots of people seated around the ring.

"What sort of things do you think the judges are looking for?" James asked her.

"I asked Mrs Talbot that," Mandy replied. "She said they're not just interested in the best-looking cows, they have to be really healthy too. So they look at their udders, and their coats."

"None of the other cows are going to have shinier coats than Jenny and Tilly." James grinned. "I groomed Jenny for so long, my arm nearly fell off!"

"Ladies and gentlemen, boys and girls, welcome to the Rare Breeds classes," a voice announced over the tannoy. "And first into the ring, we have the Dexter cows with calf at foot."

Mandy sat forward in her seat as the cows and their calves were led out in a long line. At the front was Rob Talbot, leading Buttercup, followed by a woman Mandy had never seen before leading Tansy. Mandy guessed she was Rob's wife. She bobbed up and down in her seat, trying to catch a glimpse of Jenny and Tilly, but they were further down the line.

Here they were now! Mandy turned and grinned at James as she spotted Mike and Jenny, with Rachel and Tilly behind them. Jenny was walking calmly beside Mike, and Mandy thought proudly that she and Tilly were definitely the best-looking cow and calf in the ring. She couldn't see how the judges could give the champion's sash to anyone else!

Tilly, too, was attracting a lot of attention. People started whispering and pointing at her as the calf walked round, and Mandy heard several people behind her saying how beautiful Tilly was.

Now it was time for the cows and their calves to line up in the middle of the ring, so that the judges could take a closer look at them. Mandy and James watched as Mike and Rachel took their place in the line. Then they had to wait while the judges made their way slowly down the row, looking at the cows' eyes and udders and flanks.

Suddenly Jenny gave a loud moo that made Mandy almost jump out of her seat. A second later, Jenny jerked forward sharply, yanking the lead rope right out of Mike's hand. As Mike

gave a shout of surprise, Jenny charged forward, straight towards the people sitting on the other side of the ring.

"Oh!" Mandy gasped in horror, jumping to her feet.

The people in the audience started to yell and scramble out of their seats as Jenny ran towards them. Some of the mothers clutched their children, trying to pull them out of the way. Everyone looked very frightened.

"James, what's going on?" Mandy could hardly believe her eyes. She could understand why people were scared. They didn't know that Jenny was sweet and good-natured, and her horns *did* look very sharp. But why on earth had Jenny suddenly taken off like that?

James shook his head. "I don't know what she's up to."

They watched anxiously as Mike chased after Jenny. Meanwhile, they could see that Tilly was getting restless, and pulling at the lead rope, trying to follow her mum.

"What do you think is going to happen now?" James asked anxiously.

Mandy bit her lip. She looked at the judges,

who were standing in a huddle, grimly shaking their heads. "Oh, James," she said in a wobbly voice. "I think Jenny's going to be disqualified!

9

Some brilliant detective work!

"Disqualified!" James gasped. "That's not fair! Won't they give her another chance?"

"I don't know," Mandy replied. She felt very upset. And what about poor Mr and Mrs Talbot? Mandy felt very sorry for them.

Mike tore across the ring and managed to grab Jenny's lead rope just before she reached the first row of seats. He dug in his heels and pulled her to a stop.

His face was grim as he stroked Jenny's neck and made her stand quietly beside him. His wife was still holding Tilly, and she looked shocked and miserable. Neither of them looked as if they could believe what had just happened.

Mandy's head was spinning. It just didn't make sense. Jenny had been in the ring before. It wasn't as if it was her first show, and she'd got scared. There *had* to be a reason.

The judges walked over to Mike and Jenny. They looked quite stern-faced, and Mandy guessed with a sinking feeling that Jenny was about to be disqualified. Surely there was something they could do, Mandy thought desperately. She stared across at the seats opposite them. Maybe she could work out what had made Jenny run towards them like that.

All of a sudden, she spotted the curly-haired boy that Rob Talbot had been talking to. As Mike led Jenny back into the line of cows, the boy got up from his seat at the front of the show-ring. Glancing right and left, as if he was making sure that no one was watching him, he slipped quietly away.

Mandy frowned. Jenny had run right towards
that particular seat. She nudged James. "You
remember that boy who was talking to Rob
Talbot?" she said in a low voice.

James nodded, looking puzzled. The judges
were talking to Mike, their faces very stern.
But the audience laughed when Tilly, who was
obviously feeling hungry, butted her head into
Jenny's flank and began to suck hungrily from
her mum.

"He was sitting over there," Mandy went on,

99

pointing at the seats opposite them. "Jenny ran straight towards him."

James stared at her. "Do you think he might have had something to do with it?" he asked.

"Maybe," Mandy said, feeling a bit uncertain. "But I don't know what."

James squinted across the ring. "Well, I can't see him now."

"He just got up and walked off," Mandy explained. "I think we ought to go after him."

James looked doubtful. "But what are we going to tell Mrs Todd?"

"We'll think of something," Mandy said. She looked round to see if she could spot where the boy had gone. Then her eyes opened wide. The boy was making his way towards *their* side of the ring!

The boy came closer, searching for an empty seat. Now Mandy could see the plastic bag sticking out of his pocket. And what were those brown crumbs on the boy's sweatshirt? They looked familiar.

She nudged James. "I wonder what's in that bag?" she whispered.

One of the judges who had been speaking to Mike was now pointing towards the exit. Mandy's heart sank right down to her shoes. Jenny had been disqualified!

"Wait here," James said in a determined voice. He jumped to his feet and hurried off.

Mandy had no idea what James was planning to do. She looked anxiously at Mrs Todd, hoping the teacher wouldn't tell him to sit down again. But Mrs Todd's gaze, like everyone else's, was fixed on what was happening in the ring. People in the crowd muttered and whispered to each other as Mike led Jenny slowly towards the exit, followed by his wife and Tilly. The Talbots looked very downhearted indeed.

Meanwhile, James was walking straight towards the curly-haired boy. Mandy watched in amazement as suddenly James swerved and bumped right into him. The plastic bag fell out of the boy's pocket and landed on the ground.

"Oh, sorry," James said politely. He bent down to pick up the bag and handed it to the boy. Then he turned round and rushed back to Mandy.

"Mandy, you'll never guess what!" he gasped, as soon as he got near. "There were cattle nuts in that bag."

"Jenny's favourite snack!" Mandy's eyes opened wide. "That's what those brown crumbs on his jacket were. Somehow Jenny must have known he had them, and that's why she tried to run towards him."

"Maybe he was feeding her earlier," James suggested, "and she recognised him."

"Quick, I've got to tell Mike." Mandy jumped to her feet. "Maybe Jenny and Tilly won't be disqualified after all!"

The Talbots, Jenny and Tilly were just leaving the ring, and the judges were about to re-start the class. Mandy knew she had to act fast. Slipping out of her seat, she ran round the side of the ring towards the Talbots.

"Mandy!" Mrs Todd called after her, sounding very surprised. "Mandy, where are you going?"

The judges were looking annoyed. "Please go back to your seat immediately!" one of them called.

Mandy hurried over to Mike Talbot. "James

and I think we know why Jenny ran off like that," she panted. "That boy over there —" she turned and pointed across the ring at him, "— has got cattle nuts in his pocket. We think he might have been feeding Jenny before, and that's why she ran towards him. Maybe he knew how greedy Jenny can be."

Mike stared at the boy, then he glanced at his wife. "That's Ian Talbot," he said. "My brother Rob's son." He frowned. "There's something very strange going on here!"

10

And the winner is . . .

"What are you going to do?" Mrs Talbot asked her husband anxiously. "Do you really think Rob would do something like this on purpose?"

Mike shook his head. "I don't know," he said. "Maybe he's more desperate to win the class than I thought."

One of the judges – a small, round man with glasses – hurried over to them, looking very cross. "Your cow and calf have been disqualified, Mr Talbot," he said briskly. "And you have been asked to leave the ring. Please go immediately so that we can carry on with the class. As for you, young lady," he glanced at Mandy, "please go back to your seat."

"Just a moment, Mr Wentworth," Mike cut in. "There's something I need to tell you."

Mandy listened anxiously as Mike explained what they thought had happened. Would the judges change their minds, and let Jenny and Tilly compete in the class after all?

But Mr Wentworth shook his head slowly when Mike had finished. "That's a very serious charge, Mr Talbot," he said solemnly. "Have you got any proof?"

"If you would just let me speak to Ian before you carry on with the class," Mike pleaded. "We can get to the bottom of this."

"Actually, it's me you want to speak to," muttered a low voice behind them. "It's all my fault."

Mandy looked round. Rob Talbot was standing there, looking very shame-faced. He had given Buttercup's lead rope to his wife, and come over to where they were standing.

"You can leave Ian out of it," Rob went on. "He didn't want to do it. It was my idea."

Mandy remembered how Ian had seemed reluctant to listen to his dad when she and James had seen them by the refreshments tent.

Mike stared at his brother. "So what did you do?"

Rob couldn't look Mike in the eye. "I gave Ian some cattle nuts and sent him to the tent when you went back to your truck," he mumbled. "I told Ian to give them to Jenny, then get a seat close to the ring. I hoped she'd spot Ian and go over to him for more nuts."

"Which she did," Mike said grimly.

"I saw you looking and pointing at Ian just now," Rob explained. "And I knew that you'd worked out what happened."

"Well!" said Mr Wentworth, looking very shocked. "I've never heard of such a thing!"

"But why did you do it, Rob?" asked Rachel.

Mandy looked at Rob Talbot, and saw his face drop. "My farm's doing pretty badly at the moment," he confessed gloomily. "I thought that if I could win this class, I'd get some good publicity out if it."

"Oh!" Mandy suddenly thought of something. She looked at James, sitting by the ring, then reached up on tiptoe and whispered to Mike, "I wonder if it was Mr Talbot who hid Jenny in the shelter?"

Mike glared at his brother. "Was it *you* who took Jenny when she disappeared last week?" he asked.

Rob nodded. "But I would have brought her back safely after the show," he said earnestly. "I only wanted Buttercup to win, I would never have hurt Jenny. You've got to believe me."

Mike nodded. "I do believe you," he said. "And Jenny didn't come to any harm."

Mandy couldn't help feeling sorry for Rob now that they'd heard the whole story. Meanwhile, the crowd was getting restless, wondering what was going on. Mandy caught James's eye. He looked as if he was going to burst if he didn't find out what was happening! And, further along the row of seats, Ian Talbot was looking very worried.

Rob turned to Mr Wentworth. "I suppose I'm disqualified now?" he said quietly.

Mr Wentworth sighed. "I'm afraid so. Mike, would you like to bring Jenny and Tilly back into the ring?"

"You mean, Jenny and Tilly aren't disqualified?" Mandy exclaimed.

Mr Wentworth smiled at her. "No, they're not," he said. "And now it's about time you went back to your seat!"

Mandy nodded, and ran back towards James.

"Mandy, what on earth is going on?" asked Mrs Todd.

"What's happened?" demanded James.

"It's all right," Mandy gasped, her eyes shining with relief. "Jenny and Tilly are back in the class!"

She didn't get a chance to say anything more, because there was an announcement over the tannoy. "Treetop Jenny and Treetop Tilly will be taking part in the class after all," said the steward. "However, Lowfell Buttercup and Lowfell Tansy have been disqualified."

Ian Talbot, looking very pale, jumped up out of his seat and hurried off.

"So we were right!" said James, sounding pleased.

Mandy nodded. "I'll tell you the rest later," she whispered, as the judging began again.

This time both Jenny and Tilly behaved beautifully. They waited quietly in line for the judges to come along and look at them. Jenny had a good sniff at Mr Wentworth's pockets as he felt her smooth coat, which made the audience laugh. Soon the judges had walked along the whole line of cows. Then they moved a short distance away to discuss the competitors and decide on a winner.

"Come on," muttered James. "Why is it taking so long?"

Mandy could hardly sit still as she waited for the winner to be announced. Surely it would be Jenny and Tilly – or would Jenny's previous bad behaviour still count against her?

Mr Wentworth was holding the champion's sash. Mandy held her breath as the judge walked towards the line of cows and calves. Which pair was he heading towards?

Mr Wentworth stopped beside Jenny and Tilly. He said a few words to Mr and Mrs Talbot – then he slipped the purple and gold sash over Jenny's head!

"And the winners of the Dexter Cow and Calf Class this year are Jenny and her calf Tilly, who are owned by Mr and Mrs Talbot of Treetop Farm!" the voice over the tannoy announced. "Jenny is our winner for the third year running. She's obviously a very special cow indeed!"

Mandy and James couldn't have agreed more. They clapped until their hands were sore, while

Mike and his wife led Jenny and Tilly on a victory lap around the ring. Everyone laughed as Tilly gently headbutted Mr Wentworth when they walked past him. It looked as if she was saying *Thank you*!

"Mrs Todd, please could we go and see Jenny and Tilly?" Mandy asked. "We'll be very quick."

Mrs Todd smiled. "I don't know what's been going on, but I'm sure you'll let me know later!" she said. "Off you go, but don't be too long."

Mandy and James jumped out of their seats and raced round to the ring entrance. Mike and Rachel were standing there with Jenny and Tilly. They were talking to Rob Talbot, who was still looking rather ashamed of himself. Ian was standing next to his father, looking uncomfortable. Mandy and James didn't want to interrupt, so they stood at one side and made a fuss of Tilly and Jenny.

"You were both great!" Mandy whispered in Tilly's ear. But Jenny was more interested in trying to chew the winner's sash that hung round her neck.

"You can't eat *that*, Jenny!" laughed James.

"Tilly's lovely, isn't she?" said a quiet voice behind them. Mandy turned round to see Ian Talbot staring shyly at the cows. He leaned over and patted Tilly's head. "She really deserved to win."

"Tansy's very pretty, too," Mandy replied.

"Congratulations, Mike and Rachel!" Alison West was hurrying towards them, holding her camera. "I'm going to need some pictures for the newspaper. But why were your cow and calf disqualified, Mr Talbot?" she asked, turning to Rob Talbot.

Rob looked embarrassed.

"Oh, it wasn't anything important," Mike cut in. Rob looked at him gratefully. "I've got something much more interesting to tell you, Alison."

"Oh?" Alison flipped open her notebook.

Mandy wondered what Mike was going to say.

"This is the last year that my brother and I will be competing against each other," Mike went on. "We've decided to combine our two farms, and work together. So next year, the

Talbots will be on the same side!"

Rob and Ian looked very pleased, and so did Mike and Rachel. Mandy and James grinned at each other. Mike had obviously decided that this was the best way he could help his brother out.

"Right, how about that photo then?" said Mike. "And I think Mandy and James should be in it too. They've been *really* helpful." He winked at them.

So Mandy stood next to Mrs Talbot and Tilly, while James stood next to Jenny and Mike. They just about managed to stop Jenny from chewing on her champion's sash while the picture was taken.

"We're going to have a lot to write in our project tomorrow, aren't we?" James whispered in Mandy's ear.

Mandy laughed as she gave Tilly a hug. "Oh, yes!" she said. "Who would have thought so much could happen in just one Cow and Calf class?"

LUCY DANIELS

Animal Ark Pets 2
Kitten Crowd

Mandy Hope loves animals and knows lots about them too – both her parents are vets! So Mandy's always able to help her friends with their pet problems . . .

Mandy's friend Katie had six newborn kittens to look after – but her family are moving house and they can't take the kittens with them.

Can Mandy find a new home for them all – by the end of the week?

RAT RIDDLE
Animal Ark Pets 18

Lucy Daniels

Mandy and James's school-friend Martin has been given a pair of fancy rats for his birthday. Cheddar and Pickle love to race around their 'Incredible Rat Run'. At first, Mandy finds that Pickle is the fastest. But then Pickle's times begin to slow down. Could something be wrong?

FOAL FROLICS
Animal Ark Pets Summer Special

Lucy Daniels

Mandy and James are on holiday with Mandy's family. All sorts of things are disappearing from the campsite, and now golf balls from the nearby golf course are going missing too. It's a mystery until Mandy and James catch the thief red-handed: a cheeky foal called Mischief! The bad-tempered groundsman at the golf course wants Mischief removed. Can Mandy and James find a way for the foal to stay?

LUCY DANIELS

Animal Ark Pets

0 340 67283 8	Puppy Puzzle	£3.99	☐
0 340 67284 6	Kitten Crowd	£3.99	☐
0 340 67285 4	Rabbit Race	£3.99	☐
0 340 67286 2	Hamster Hotel	£3.99	☐
0 340 68729 0	Mouse Magic	£3.99	☐
0 340 68730 4	Chick Challenge	£3.99	☐
0 340 68731 2	Pony Parade	£3.99	☐
0 340 68732 0	Guinea-pig Gang	£3.99	☐
0 340 71371 2	Gerbil Genius	£3.99	☐
0 340 71372 0	Duckling Diary	£3.99	☐
0 340 71373 9	Lamb Lessons	£3.99	☐
0 340 71374 7	Doggy Dare	£3.99	☐
0 340 73585 6	Donkey Derby	£3.99	☐
0 340 73586 4	Hedgehog Home	£3.99	☐
0 340 73587 2	Frog Friends	£3.99	☐
0 340 73588 0	Bunny Bonanza	£3.99	☐
0 340 73589 9	Ferret Fun	£3.99	☐
0 340 73590 2	Rat Riddle	£3.99	☐
0 340 73592 9	Cat Crazy	£3.99	☐
0 340 73605 4	Pets' Party	£3.99	☐
0 340 73593 7	Foal Frolics	£3.99	☐
0 340 77861 X	Piglet Pranks	£3.99	☐
0 340 77878 4	Spaniel Surprise	£3.99	☐
0 340 85204 6	Horse Hero	£3.99	☐
0 340 85205 4	Calf Capers	£3.99	☐
0 340 85206 2	Puppy Prizes	£3.99	☐

All Hodder Children's books are available at your local bookshop, or can be ordered direct from the publisher. Just tick the titles you would like and complete the details below. Prices and availability are subject to change without prior notice.

Please enclose a cheque or postal order made payable to *Bookpoint Ltd*, and send to: Hodder Children's Books, 39 Milton Park, Abingdon, OXON OX14 4TD, UK. Email Address: orders@bookpoint.co.uk

If you would prefer to pay by credit card, our call centre team would be delighted to take your order by telephone. Our direct line *01235 400414* (lines open 9.00 am–6.00 pm Monday to Saturday, 24 hour message answering service). Alternatively you can send a fax on *01235 400454*.

TITLE		FIRST NAME		SURNAME	

ADDRESS	
DAYTIME TEL:	POST CODE

If you would prefer to pay by credit card, please complete:
Please debit my Visa/Access/Diner's Card/American Express (delete as applicable) card no:

Signature .... Expiry Date: ....

If you would NOT like to receive further information on our products please tick the box. ☐